Praise for J.K

THE TALES OF

BEEDLE
THE BARD

'Refreshingly original ... and surprisingly satisfying'
Sunday Times

'The five enchanting tales told with the author's
confident mixture of wit and wariness tell lessons
for both children and parents alike'
Sunday Express

'The tales drip with the brash, ironic humour
familiar to Potter readers'
Financial Times

'An intricate in-joke complete with footnotes
that will engross any close student of Harry Potter'
Observer

'The stories are original, diverse, witty
and wise ... a storytelling treat'
Books for Keeps

THE TALES OF
BEEDLE
THE BARD

THE HARRY POTTER SERIES

In reading order:
Harry Potter and the Philosopher's Stone
Harry Potter and the Chamber of Secrets
Harry Potter and the Prisoner of Azkaban
Harry Potter and the Goblet of Fire
Harry Potter and the Order of the Phoenix
Harry Potter and the Half-Blood Prince
Harry Potter and the Deathly Hallows

Also available in Latin:
Harry Potter and the Philosopher's Stone
Harry Potter and the Chamber of Secrets

Also available in Welsh, Ancient Greek and Irish:
Harry Potter and the Philosopher's Stone

ILLUSTRATED EDITIONS

Illustrated by Jim Kay
Harry Potter and the Philosopher's Stone
Harry Potter and the Chamber of Secrets

COMPANION VOLUMES

Fantastic Beasts and Where to Find Them
Quidditch Through the Ages
(Published in aid of Comic Relief)

The Tales of Beedle the Bard
(Published in aid of Lumos)

The three companion volumes also available as:
The Hogwarts Library
(Published in aid of Comic Relief and Lumos)

J.K. ROWLING

THE TALES OF
BEEDLE
THE BARD

Translated from the original
runes by Hermione Granger

With additional notes by
Professor Albus Dumbledore

BLOOMSBURY
LONDON OXFORD NEW YORK NEW DELHI SYDNEY

LUMOS
Protecting Children. Providing Solutions.

Bloomsbury Publishing, London, Oxford, New York, New Delhi and Sydney

First published in Great Britain in 2008 by Lumos (formerly the Children's High Level Group),
Gredley House, 1–11 Broadway, London E15 4BQ,
in association with Bloomsbury Publishing Plc
50 Bedford Square, London WC1B 3DP

Bloomsbury is a registered trademark of Bloomsbury Publishing Plc

This edition published in 2017

Text design by Becky Chilcott

Lumos and the Lumos logo and associated logos
are trademarks of the Lumos Foundation

Lumos is the operating name of Lumos Foundation (formerly the Children's High Level Group).
It is a company limited by guarantee registered in England and Wales, number: 5611912.
Registered charity number: 1112575

A CIP catalogue record of this book is available from the British Library

HARDBACK ISBN 978 1 4088 8072 2
1 3 5 7 9 10 8 6 4 2

PAPERBACK ISBN 978 1 4088 8309 9
1 3 5 7 9 10 8 6 4 2

Printed and bound in Great Britain by CPI Group (UK) Ltd, Croydon CR0 4YY

www.wearelumos.org
www.pottermore.com
www.bloomsbury.com

Contents

Introduction

THE TALES OF BEEDLE THE BARD is a collection of stories written for young wizards and witches. They have been popular bedtime reading for centuries, with the result that the Hopping Pot and the Fountain of Fair Fortune are as familiar to many of the students at Hogwarts as Cinderella and Sleeping Beauty are to Muggle (non-magical) children.

Beedle's stories resemble our fairy tales in many respects; for instance, virtue is usually rewarded and wickedness punished. However, there is one very obvious difference. In Muggle fairy tales, magic tends to lie at the root of the hero or heroine's troubles – the wicked witch has poisoned the apple, or put the princess into a hundred years' sleep, or turned the prince into a hideous beast. In *The Tales of Beedle the Bard*, on the other hand, we meet heroes and heroines who can perform magic themselves, and yet find it just as hard to solve their problems as we do. Beedle's stories have helped generations of wizarding parents to explain this painful fact of life to their young children: that magic causes as much trouble as it cures.

Another notable difference between these fables and their Muggle counterparts is that Beedle's witches are much more active in seeking their fortunes than our fairy-tale heroines. Asha, Altheda, Amata and Babbitty Rabbitty are all witches who take their fate into their own hands, rather than taking a prolonged nap or waiting for someone to return a lost shoe. The exception to this rule – the unnamed maiden of 'The Warlock's Hairy Heart' – acts more like our idea of a storybook princess, but there is no 'happily ever after' at the end of her tale.

Beedle the Bard lived in the fifteenth century and much of his life remains shrouded in mystery. We know that he was born in Yorkshire, and the only surviving woodcut shows that he had an exceptionally luxuriant beard. If his stories accurately reflect his opinions, he rather liked Muggles, whom he regarded as ignorant rather than malevolent; he mistrusted Dark Magic, and he believed that the worst excesses of wizardkind sprang from the all-too-human traits of cruelty, apathy or arrogant misapplication of their own talents. The heroes and heroines who triumph in his stories are not those with the most powerful magic, but rather those who demonstrate the most kindness, common sense and ingenuity.

One modern-day wizard who held very similar views was, of course, Professor Albus Percival Wulfric Brian Dumbledore, Order of Merlin, First Class, Headmaster of Hogwarts School of Witchcraft and Wizardry, Supreme Mugwump of the International Confederation of Wizards, and Chief Warlock of the Wizengamot. This similarity of outlook notwithstanding, it was a surprise to discover a set of notes on

The Tales of Beedle the Bard among the many papers that Dumbledore left in his will to the Hogwarts Archives. Whether this commentary was written for his own satisfaction, or for future publication, we shall never know; however, we have been graciously granted permission by Professor Minerva McGonagall, now Headmistress of Hogwarts, to print Professor Dumbledore's notes here, alongside a brand new translation of the tales by Hermione Granger. We hope that Professor Dumbledore's insights, which include observations on wizarding history, personal reminiscences and enlightening information on key elements of each story, will help a new generation of both wizarding and Muggle readers appreciate *The Tales of Beedle the Bard*. It is the belief of all who knew him personally that Professor Dumbledore would have been delighted to lend his support to this project, given that all royalties are to be donated to Lumos, a charity which works to benefit children in desperate need of a voice.

It seems only right to make one small, additional comment on Professor Dumbledore's notes. As far as we can tell, the notes were completed around eighteen months before the tragic events that took place at the top of Hogwarts' Astronomy Tower. Those familiar with the history of the most recent wizarding war (everyone who has read all seven volumes on the life of Harry Potter, for instance) will be aware that Professor Dumbledore reveals a little less than he knows – or suspects – about the final story in this book. The reason for any omission lies, perhaps, in what Dumbledore said about truth, many years ago, to his favourite and most famous pupil:

'It is a beautiful and terrible thing, and should therefore be treated with great caution.'

Whether we agree with him or not, we can perhaps excuse Professor Dumbledore for wishing to protect future readers from the temptations to which he himself had fallen prey, and for which he paid so terrible a price.

JK Rowling
2008

A Note on the Footnotes

Professor Dumbledore appears to have been writing for a wizarding audience, so I have occasionally inserted an explanation of a term or fact that might need clarification for Muggle readers.

JKR

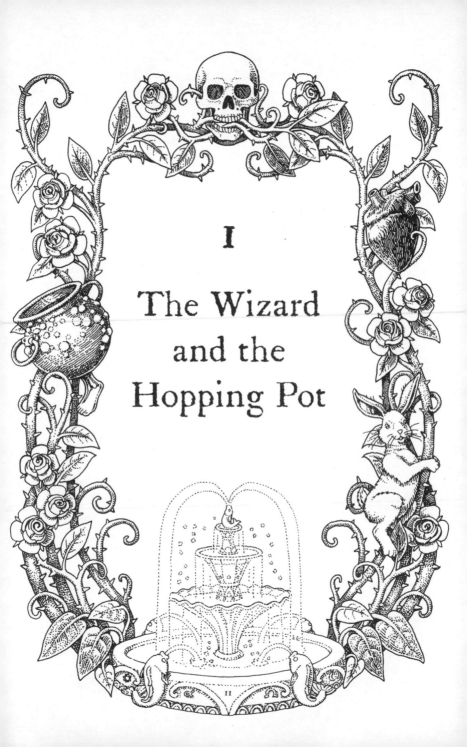

I

The Wizard and the Hopping Pot

THERE WAS ONCE A KINDLY old wizard
who used his magic generously and wisely for
the benefit of his neighbours. Rather than reveal the
true source of his power, he pretended that his
potions, charms and antidotes sprang ready-made
from the little cauldron he called his lucky cooking
pot. From miles around people came to him with
their troubles, and the wizard was pleased to give his
pot a stir and put things right.

This well-beloved wizard lived to a goodly age,
then died, leaving all his chattels to his only son.
This son was of a very different disposition to his
gentle father. Those who could not work magic

were, to the son's mind, worthless, and he had often quarrelled with his father's habit of dispensing magical aid to their neighbours.

Upon the father's death, the son found hidden inside the old cooking pot a small package bearing his name. He opened it, hoping for gold, but found instead a soft, thick slipper, much too small to wear, and with no pair. A fragment of parchment within the slipper bore the words 'In the fond hope, my son, that you will never need it.'

The son cursed his father's age-softened mind, then threw the slipper back into the cauldron, resolving to use it henceforth as a rubbish pail.

That very night a peasant woman knocked on the front door.

'My granddaughter is afflicted by a crop of warts, sir,' she told him. 'Your father used to mix a special poultice in that old cooking pot –'

'Begone!' cried the son. 'What care I for your brat's warts?'

And he slammed the door in the old woman's face.

At once there came a loud clanging and banging from his kitchen. The wizard lit his wand and opened the door, and there, to his amazement, he saw his father's old cooking pot: it had sprouted a single foot of brass, and was hopping on the spot, in the middle of the floor, making a fearful noise upon the flagstones. The wizard approached

it in wonder, but fell back hurriedly when he saw that the whole of the pot's surface was covered in warts.

'Disgusting object!' he cried, and he tried firstly to Vanish the pot, then to clean it by magic, and finally to force it out of the house. None of his spells worked, however, and he was unable to prevent the pot hopping after him out of the kitchen, and then following him up to bed, clanging and banging loudly on every wooden stair.

The wizard could not sleep all night for the banging of the warty old pot by his bedside, and next morning the pot insisted upon hopping after him to the breakfast table. *Clang, clang, clang,* went the brass-footed pot, and the wizard had not even started his porridge when there came another knock on the door.

An old man stood on the doorstep.

'''Tis my old donkey, sir,' he explained. 'Lost, she is, or stolen, and without her I cannot take my wares to market, and my family will go hungry tonight.'

'And I am hungry now!' roared the wizard, and he slammed the door upon the old man.

Clang, clang, clang,
went the cooking pot's
single brass foot upon the
floor, but now its clamour
was mixed with the brays of
a donkey and human groans
of hunger, echoing from the
depths of the pot.

'Be still. Be silent!' shrieked the wizard, but not
all his magical powers could quieten the warty pot,
which hopped at his heels all day, braying and
groaning and clanging, no matter where he went or
what he did.

That evening there came a third
knock upon the door, and there
on the threshold stood a young
woman sobbing as though her
heart would break.

'My baby is grievously
ill,' she said. 'Won't you please
help us? Your father bade me
come if troubled –'

But the wizard slammed the door on her.

And now the tormenting pot filled to the brim with salt water, and slopped tears all over the floor as it hopped, and brayed, and groaned, and sprouted more warts.

Though no more villagers came to seek help at the wizard's cottage for the rest of the week, the pot kept him informed of their many ills. Within a few days, it was not only braying and groaning and slopping and hopping and sprouting warts, it was also choking and retching, crying like a baby, whining like a dog, and spewing out bad cheese and sour milk and a plague of hungry slugs.

The wizard could not sleep or eat with the pot beside him, but the pot refused to leave, and he could not silence it or force it to be still.

At last the wizard could bear it no more.

'Bring me all your problems, all your troubles and your woes!' he screamed, fleeing into the night,

with the pot hopping behind him along the road into the village. 'Come! Let me cure you, mend you and comfort you! I have my father's cooking pot, and I shall make you well!'

And with the foul pot still bounding along behind him, he ran up the street, casting spells in every direction.

Inside one house the little girl's warts vanished as she slept; the lost donkey was Summoned from a distant briar patch and set down softly in its stable; the sick baby was doused in dittany and woke, well and rosy. At every house of sickness and sorrow, the wizard did his best, and gradually the cooking pot beside him stopped groaning and retching, and became quiet, shiny and clean.

'Well, Pot?' asked the trembling wizard, as the sun began to rise.

The pot burped out the single slipper he had thrown into it, and permitted him to fit it on to the brass foot. Together, they set off back to the wizard's house, the pot's footstep muffled at last. But from that day forward, the wizard helped the villagers like his father before him, lest the pot cast off its slipper, and begin to hop once more.

Albus Dumbledore on
'The Wizard and the
Hopping Pot'

A kind old wizard decides to teach his hard-hearted son a lesson by giving him a taste of the local Muggles' misery. The young wizard's conscience awakes, and he agrees to use his magic for the benefit of his non-magical neighbours. A simple and heart-warming fable, one might think – in which case, one would reveal oneself to be an innocent nincompoop. A pro-Muggle story showing a Muggle-loving father as superior in magic to a Muggle-hating son? It is nothing short of amazing that any copies of the original version of this tale survived the flames to which they were so often consigned.

Beedle was somewhat out of step with his times in preaching a message of brotherly love for Muggles. The persecution of witches and wizards was gathering pace all over Europe in the early fifteenth century. Many in the magical community felt, and with good reason, that offering to cast a spell on the Muggle-next-door's sickly pig was tantamount to volunteering to fetch the firewood for one's own funeral pyre.[1] 'Let the Muggles manage without us!' was the cry, as the wizards drew further and further apart from their non-magical brethren, culminating with the institution of the International Statute of Wizarding

---

[1]. It is true, of course, that genuine witches and wizards were reasonably adept at escaping the stake, block and noose (see my comments about Lisette de Lapin in the commentary on 'Babbitty Rabbitty and her Cackling Stump'). However, a number of deaths did occur: Sir Nicholas de Mimsy-Porpington (a wizard at the royal court in his lifetime, and in his death-time, ghost of Gryffindor Tower) was stripped of his wand before being locked in a dungeon, and was unable to magic himself out of his execution; and wizarding families were particularly prone to losing younger members, whose inability to control their own magic made them noticeable, and vulnerable, to Muggle witch-hunters.

Secrecy in 1689, when wizardkind voluntarily went underground.

Children being children, however, the grotesque Hopping Pot had taken hold of their imaginations. The solution was to jettison the pro-Muggle moral but keep the warty cauldron, so by the middle of the sixteenth century a different version of the tale was in wide circulation among wizarding families. In the revised story, the Hopping Pot protects an innocent wizard from his torch-bearing, pitchfork-toting neighbours by chasing them away from the wizard's cottage, catching them and swallowing them whole. At the end of the story, by which time the Pot has consumed most of his neighbours, the wizard gains a promise from the few remaining villagers that he will be left in peace to practise magic. In return, he instructs the Pot to render up its victims, who are duly burped out of its depths, slightly mangled. To this day, some wizarding children are only told the revised version of the story by their (generally anti-Muggle) parents, and the original, if and when they ever read it, comes as a great surprise.

As I have already hinted, however, its pro-Muggle sentiment was not the only reason that 'The Wizard and the Hopping Pot' attracted anger. As the witch-hunts grew ever fiercer, wizarding families began to live double lives, using charms of concealment to protect themselves and their families. By the seventeenth century, any witch or wizard who chose to fraternise with Muggles became suspect, even an outcast in his or her own community. Among the many insults hurled at pro-Muggle witches and wizards (such fruity epithets as 'Mudwallower', 'Dunglicker' and 'Scumsucker' date from this period) was the charge of having weak or inferior magic.

Influential wizards of the day, such as Brutus Malfoy, editor of *Warlock at War*, an anti-Muggle periodical, perpetuated the stereotype that a Muggle-lover was about as magical as a Squib.[2] In 1675, Brutus wrote:

This we may state with certainty: any wizard

---

2. [A Squib is a person born to magical parents, but who has no magical powers. Such an occurrence is rare. Muggle-born witches and wizards are much more common. JKR]

who shows fondness for the society of Muggles is
of low intelligence, with magic so feeble and
pitiful that he can only feel himself superior if
surrounded by Muggle pigmen.

Nothing is a surer sign of weak magic than
a weakness for non-magical company.

This prejudice eventually died out in the face of overwhelming evidence that some of the world's most brilliant wizards[3] were, to use the common phrase, 'Muggle-lovers'.

The final objection to 'The Wizard and the Hopping Pot' remains alive in certain quarters today. It was summed up best, perhaps, by Beatrix Bloxam (1794–1910), author of the infamous *Toadstool Tales*. Mrs Bloxam believed that *The Tales of Beedle the Bard* were damaging to children because of what she called 'their unhealthy preoccupation with the most horrid subjects, such as death, disease, bloodshed, wicked magic, unwholesome characters and bodily effusions and eruptions of the most disgusting kind'.

---

3. Such as myself.

Mrs Bloxam took a variety of old stories, including several of Beedle's, and rewrote them according to her ideals, which she expressed as 'filling the pure minds of our little angels with healthy, happy thoughts, keeping their sweet slumber free of wicked dreams and protecting the precious flower of their innocence'.

The final paragraph of Mrs Bloxam's pure and precious reworking of 'The Wizard and the Hopping Pot' reads:

Then the little golden pot danced with delight – hoppitty hoppitty hop! – on its tiny rosy toes! Wee Willykins had cured all the dollies of their poorly tum-tums, and the little pot was so happy that it filled up with sweeties for Wee Willykins and the dollies!

'But don't forget to brush your teethy-pegs!' cried the pot.

And Wee Willykins kissed and huggled the hoppitty pot and promised always to help the dollies and never to be an old grumpy-wumpkins again.

Mrs Bloxam's tale has met the same response from generations of wizarding children: uncontrollable retching, followed by an immediate demand to have the book taken from them and mashed into pulp.

2

The
Fountain of
Fair Fortune

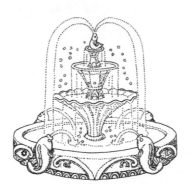

HIGH ON A HILL IN an enchanted garden, enclosed by tall walls and protected by strong magic, flowed the Fountain of Fair Fortune.

Once a year, between the hours of sunrise and sunset on the longest day, a single unfortunate was given the chance to fight their way to the Fountain, bathe in its waters and receive Fair Fortune for evermore.

On the appointed day, hundreds of people travelled from all over the kingdom to reach the garden walls before dawn. Male and female, rich and poor, young and old, of magical means and without, they gathered in the darkness, each hoping that they would be the one to gain entrance to the garden.

Three witches, each with her burden of woe, met on the outskirts of the crowd, and told one another their sorrows as they waited for sunrise.

The first, by name Asha, was sick of a malady no Healer could cure. She hoped that the Fountain would banish her symptoms and grant her a long and happy life.

The second, by name Altheda, had been robbed of her home, her gold and her wand by an evil sorcerer. She hoped that the Fountain might relieve her of powerlessness and poverty.

The third, by name Amata, had been deserted by a man whom she loved dearly, and she thought her heart would never mend. She hoped that the Fountain would relieve her of her grief and longing.

Pitying each other, the three women agreed that, should the chance befall them, they would unite and try to reach the Fountain together.

The sky was rent with the first ray of sun, and a chink in the wall opened. The crowd surged forward, each of them shrieking their claim for the Fountain's benison. Creepers from the garden beyond snaked through the pressing mass, and twisted themselves around the first witch, Asha. She grasped the wrist of the second witch, Altheda, who seized tight upon the robes of the third witch, Amata.

And Amata became caught upon the armour of a dismal-looking knight who was seated on a bone-thin horse.

The creepers tugged the three witches through the chink in the wall, and the knight was dragged off his steed after them.

The furious screams of the disappointed throng rose upon the morning air, then fell silent as the garden walls sealed once more.

Asha and Altheda were angry with Amata, who
had accidentally brought along the knight.

'Only one can bathe in the Fountain! It will be
hard enough to decide which of us it will be, without
adding another!'

Now, Sir Luckless, as the knight was known in
the land outside the walls, observed that these were
witches, and, having no magic, nor any great skill at
jousting or duelling with swords, nor anything that
distinguished the non-magical man, was sure that he
had no hope of beating the three women to the
Fountain. He therefore declared his intention of
withdrawing outside the walls again.

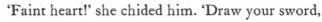

At this, Amata became angry too.

'Faint heart!' she chided him. 'Draw your sword,

Knight, and help us reach our goal!'

And so the three witches and the forlorn knight ventured forth into the enchanted garden, where rare herbs, fruit and flowers grew in abundance on either side of the sunlit paths. They met no obstacle until they reached the foot of the hill on which the Fountain stood.

There, however, wrapped around the base of the hill, was a monstrous white Worm, bloated and blind. At their approach, it turned a foul face upon them, and uttered the following words:

'Pay me the proof of your pain.'

Sir Luckless drew his sword and attempted to kill the beast, but his blade snapped. Then Altheda cast rocks at the Worm, while Asha and Amata essayed every spell that might subdue or entrance it, but the power of their wands was no more effective than their friend's stone, or the knight's steel: the Worm would not let them pass.

The sun rose higher and higher in the sky, and Asha, despairing, began to weep.

Then the great Worm placed its face upon hers and drank the tears from her cheeks. Its thirst assuaged, the Worm slithered aside, and vanished into a hole in the ground.

Rejoicing at the Worm's disappearance, the three witches and the knight began to climb the hill, sure that they would reach the Fountain before noon.

Halfway up the steep slope, however, they came across words cut into the ground before them.

Pay me the fruit of your labours.

Sir Luckless took out his only coin, and placed it upon the grassy hillside, but it rolled away and was lost. The three witches and the knight continued to climb, but though they walked for hours more, they advanced not a step; the summit came no nearer, and still the inscription lay in the earth before them.

All were discouraged as the sun rose over their heads and began to sink towards the far horizon, but Altheda walked faster and harder than any of them, and exhorted the others to follow her example, though she moved no further up the enchanted hill.

'Courage, friends, and do not yield!' she cried, wiping the sweat from her brow.

As the drops fell glittering on to the earth, the inscription blocking their path vanished, and they found that they were able to move upwards once more.

Delighted by the removal of this second obstacle, they hurried towards the summit as fast as they could, until at last they glimpsed the Fountain, glittering like crystal in a bower of flowers and trees.

Before they could reach it, however, they came to a stream that ran round the hilltop, barring their

way. In the depths of the clear water lay a smooth stone bearing the words:

Pay me the treasure of your past.

Sir Luckless attempted to float across the stream on his shield, but it sank. The three witches pulled him from the water, then tried to leap the brook themselves, but it would not let them cross, and all the while the sun was sinking lower in the sky.

So they fell to pondering the meaning of the stone's message, and Amata was the first to understand.

Taking her wand, she drew from her
mind all the memories of happy times she
had spent with her vanished lover, and dropped
them into the rushing waters. The stream swept
them away, and stepping stones appeared, and
the three witches and the knight were able to
pass at last on to the summit of the hill.

The Fountain shimmered before them,
set amidst herbs and flowers rarer and more
beautiful than any they had yet seen. The
sky burned ruby, and it was time to
decide which of them would bathe.

Before they could make their decision, however, frail Asha fell to the ground. Exhausted by their struggle to the summit, she was close to death.

Her three friends would have carried her to the Fountain, but Asha was in mortal agony and begged them not to touch her.

Then Altheda hastened to pick all those herbs she thought most hopeful, and mixed them in Sir Luckless's gourd of water, and poured the potion into Asha's mouth.

At once, Asha was able to stand. What was more, all symptoms of her dread malady had vanished.

'I am cured!' she cried. 'I have no need of the Fountain – let Altheda bathe!'

But Altheda was busy collecting more herbs in her apron.

'If I can cure this disease, I shall earn gold aplenty! Let Amata bathe!'

Sir Luckless bowed, and gestured Amata towards the Fountain, but she shook her head. The stream had washed away all regret for her lover, and she saw now that he had been cruel and faithless, and that it was happiness enough to be rid of him.

'Good sir, you must bathe, as a reward for all your chivalry!' she told Sir Luckless.

So the knight clanked forth in the last rays of the setting sun, and bathed in the Fountain of Fair Fortune, astonished that he was the chosen one of hundreds and giddy with his incredible luck.

As the sun fell below the horizon, Sir Luckless emerged from the waters with the glory of his triumph upon him, and flung himself in his rusted

armour at the feet of Amata, who was the kindest and most beautiful woman he had ever beheld. Flushed with success, he begged for her hand and her heart, and Amata, no less delighted, realised that she had found a man worthy of them.

The three witches and the knight set off down the hill together, arm in arm, and all four led long and happy lives, and none of them ever knew or suspected that the Fountain's waters carried no enchantment at all.

Albus Dumbledore on 'The Fountain of Fair Fortune

'The Fountain of Fair Fortune' is a perennial favourite, so much so that it was the subject of the sole attempt to introduce a Christmas pantomime to Hogwarts' festive celebrations.

Our then Herbology master, Professor Herbert Beery,[1] an enthusiastic devotee of amateur dramatics,

---

1. Professor Beery eventually left Hogwarts to teach at W.A.D.A. (Wizarding Academy of Dramatic Arts), where, he once confessed to me, he maintained a strong aversion to mounting performances of this particular story, believing it to be unlucky.

proposed an adaptation of this well-beloved children's tale as a Yuletide treat for staff and students. I was then a young Transfiguration teacher, and Herbert assigned me to 'special effects', which included providing a fully functioning Fountain of Fair Fortune and a miniature grassy hill, up which our three heroines and hero would appear to march, while it sank slowly into the stage and out of sight.

I think I may say, without vanity, that both my Fountain and my Hill performed the parts allotted to them with simple goodwill. Alas, that the same could not be said of the rest of the cast. Ignoring for a moment the antics of the gigantic 'Worm' provided by our Care of Magical Creatures teacher, Professor Silvanus Kettleburn, the human element proved disastrous to the show. Professor Beery, in his role of director, had been dangerously oblivious to the emotional entanglements seething under his very nose. Little did he know that the students playing Amata and Sir Luckless had been boyfriend and girlfriend until one hour before the curtain rose, at which point 'Sir Luckless' transferred his affections to 'Asha'.

Suffice it to say that our seekers after Fair Fortune never made it to the top of the Hill. The curtain had barely risen when Professor Kettleburn's 'Worm' – now revealed to be an Ashwinder[2] with an Engorgement Charm upon it – exploded in a shower of hot sparks and dust, filling the Great Hall with smoke and fragments of scenery. While the enormous fiery eggs it had laid at the foot of my Hill ignited the floorboards, 'Amata' and 'Asha' turned upon each other, duelling so fiercely that Professor Beery was caught in the crossfire, and staff had to evacuate the Hall, as the inferno now raging on stage threatened to engulf the place. The night's entertainment concluded with a packed hospital wing; it was several months before the Great Hall lost its pungent aroma of wood smoke, and even longer before Professor Beery's head reassumed its normal

---

2. See *Fantastic Beasts and Where to Find Them* for a definitive description of this curious beast. It ought never to be voluntarily introduced into a wood-panelled room, nor have an Engorgement Charm placed upon it.

proportions, and Professor Kettleburn was taken off probation.[3] Headmaster Armando Dippet imposed a blanket ban on future pantomimes, a proud non-theatrical tradition that Hogwarts continues to this day.

Our dramatic fiasco notwithstanding, 'The Fountain of Fair Fortune' is probably the most popular of Beedle's tales, although, just like 'The Wizard and the Hopping Pot', it has its detractors. More than one parent has demanded the removal of this particular tale from the Hogwarts library, including, by coincidence, a descendant of Brutus Malfoy and one-time member of the Hogwarts Board of Governors, Mr Lucius Malfoy. Mr Malfoy submitted his demand for a ban on the story in writing:

---

3. Professor Kettleburn survived no fewer than sixty-two periods of probation during his employment as Care of Magical Creatures teacher. His relations with my predecessor at Hogwarts, Professor Dippet, were always strained, Professor Dippet considering him to be somewhat reckless. By the time I became Headmaster, however, Professor Kettleburn had mellowed considerably, although there were always those who took the cynical view that with only one and a half of his original limbs remaining to him, he was forced to take life at a quieter pace.

Any work of fiction or non-fiction that depicts interbreeding between wizards and Muggles should be banned from the bookshelves of Hogwarts. I do not wish my son to be influenced into sullying the purity of his bloodline by reading stories that promote wizard–Muggle marriage.

My refusal to remove the book from the library was backed by a majority of the Board of Governors. I wrote back to Mr Malfoy, explaining my decision:

So-called pure-blood families maintain their alleged purity by disowning, banishing or lying about Muggles or Muggle-borns on their family trees. They then attempt to foist their hypocrisy upon the rest of us by asking us to ban works dealing with the truths they deny. There is not a witch or wizard in existence whose blood has not mingled with that of Muggles, and I should therefore consider it both illogical and immoral to remove works dealing with the subject from our students' store of knowledge.[4]

This exchange marked the beginning of Mr Malfoy's long campaign to have me removed from my post as Headmaster of Hogwarts, and of mine to have him removed from his position as Lord Voldemort's Favourite Death Eater.

---

4. My response prompted several further letters from Mr Malfoy, but as they consisted mainly of opprobrious remarks on my sanity, parentage and hygiene, their relevance to this commentary is remote.

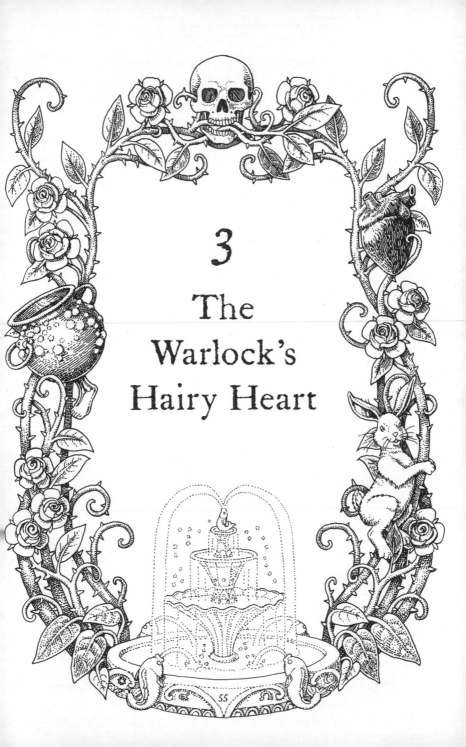

3

The Warlock's Hairy Heart

THERE WAS ONCE A HANDSOME, rich and talented young warlock, who observed that his friends grew foolish when they fell in love, gambolling and preening, losing their appetites and their dignity. The young warlock resolved never to fall prey to such weakness, and employed Dark Arts to ensure his immunity.

Unaware of his secret, the warlock's family laughed to see him so aloof and cold.

'All will change,' they prophesied, 'when a maid catches his fancy!'

But the young warlock's fancy remained untouched. Though many a maiden was intrigued by his haughty mien, and employed her most subtle arts to please him, none succeeded in touching his heart. The warlock gloried in his indifference and the sagacity that had produced it.

The first freshness of youth waned, and the warlock's peers began to wed, and then to bring forth children.

'Their hearts must be husks,' he sneered inwardly, as he observed the antics of the young parents around him, 'shrivelled by the demands of these mewling offspring!'

And once again he congratulated himself upon the wisdom of his early choice.

In due course, the warlock's aged parents died. Their son did not mourn them; on the contrary, he considered himself blessed by their demise. Now he reigned alone in their castle. Having transferred his greatest treasure to the deepest dungeon, he gave himself over to a life of ease and plenty, his comfort the only aim of his many servants.

The warlock was sure that he must be an object of immense envy to all who beheld his splendid and

untroubled solitude. Fierce were his anger and chagrin, therefore, when he overheard two of his lackeys discussing their master one day.

The first servant expressed pity for the warlock who, with all his wealth and power, was yet beloved by nobody.

But his companion jeered, asking why a man with so much gold and a palatial castle to his name had been unable to attract a wife.

Their words dealt dreadful blows to the listening warlock's pride.

He resolved at once to take a wife, and that she would be a wife superior to all others. She would possess astounding beauty, exciting envy and desire in every man who beheld her; she would spring from magical lineage, so that their offspring would inherit outstanding magical gifts; and she would have wealth at least equal to his own, so that his comfortable existence would be assured, in spite of additions to his household.

It might have taken the warlock fifty years to find such a woman, yet it so happened that the very day after he decided to seek her, a maiden answering his every wish arrived in the neighbourhood to visit her kinsfolk.

She was a witch of prodigious skill and possessed of much gold. Her beauty was such that it tugged at the heart of every man who set eyes on her; of every man, that is, except one. The warlock's heart felt nothing at all. Nevertheless, she was the prize he sought, so he began to pay her court.

All who noticed the warlock's change in manners were amazed, and told the maiden that she had succeeded where a hundred had failed.

The young woman herself was both fascinated and repelled by the warlock's attentions. She sensed the coldness that lay behind the warmth of his flattery, and had never met a man so strange and remote. Her kinsfolk, however, deemed theirs a most suitable match and, eager to promote it, accepted the warlock's invitation to a great feast in the maiden's honour.

The table was laden with silver and gold bearing the finest wines and most sumptuous foods. Minstrels

strummed on silk-stringed lutes and sang of a love their master had never felt. The maiden sat upon a throne beside the warlock, who spake low, employing words of tenderness he had stolen from the poets, without any idea of their true meaning.

The maiden listened, puzzled, and finally replied, 'You speak well, Warlock, and I would be delighted by your attentions, if only I thought you had a heart!'

The warlock smiled, and told her that she need not fear on that score. Bidding her follow, he led her from the feast, and down to the locked dungeon where he kept his greatest treasure.

Here, in an enchanted crystal casket, was the warlock's beating heart.

Long since disconnected from eyes, ears and fingers, it had never fallen prey to beauty, or to a musical voice, to the feel of silken skin. The maiden was terrified by the sight of it, for the heart was shrunken and covered in long black hair.

'Oh, what have you done?' she lamented. 'Put it back where it belongs, I beseech you!'

Seeing that this was necessary to please her, the warlock drew his wand, unlocked the crystal casket, sliced open his own breast and replaced the hairy heart in the empty cavity it had once occupied.

'Now you are healed and will know true love!' cried the maiden, and she embraced him.

The touch of her soft white arms, the sound of her breath in his ear, the scent of her heavy gold hair: all pierced the newly awakened heart like spears. But it had grown strange during its long exile, blind and savage in the darkness to which it had been condemned, and its appetites had grown powerful and perverse.

The guests at the feast had noticed the absence of their host and the maiden. At first untroubled, they grew anxious as the hours passed, and finally began to search the castle.

They found the dungeon at last, and a most dreadful sight awaited them there.

The maiden lay dead upon the floor, her breast cut open, and beside her crouched the mad warlock, holding in one bloody hand a great, smooth, shining scarlet heart, which he licked and stroked, vowing to exchange it for his own.

In his other hand, he held his wand, trying to coax from his own chest the shrivelled, hairy heart. But the hairy heart was stronger than he was, and refused to relinquish its hold upon his senses or to return to the coffin in which it had been locked for so long.

Before the horror-struck eyes of his guests, the warlock cast aside his wand, and seized a silver dagger. Vowing never to be mastered by his own heart, he hacked it from his chest.

For one moment, the warlock knelt triumphant,

with a heart clutched in each hand; then he fell across the maiden's body, and died.

Albus Dumbledore on 'The Warlock's Hairy Heart'

As we have already seen, Beedle's first two tales attracted criticism of their themes of generosity, tolerance and love. 'The Warlock's Hairy Heart', however, does not appear to have been modified or much criticised in the hundreds of years since it was first written; the story as I eventually read it in the original runes was almost exactly that which my mother had told me. That said, 'The Warlock's Hairy Heart' is by far the most gruesome of Beedle's offerings, and many parents do not share it with their children until they think they are old enough not to suffer nightmares.[1]

Why, then, the survival of this grisly tale? I would argue that 'The Warlock's Hairy Heart' has survived intact through the centuries because it speaks to the dark depths in all of us. It addresses one of the greatest, and least acknowledged, temptations of magic: the quest for invulnerability.

Of course, such a quest is nothing more or less than a foolish fantasy. No man or woman alive, magical or not, has ever escaped some form of injury, whether physical, mental or emotional. To

---

1. According to her own diary, Beatrix Bloxam never recovered from overhearing this story being told by her aunt to her older cousins. 'Quite by accident, my little ear fell against the keyhole. I can only imagine that I must have been paralysed with horror, for I inadvertently heard the whole of the disgusting story, not to mention ghastly details of the dreadfully unsavoury affair of my uncle Nobby, the local hag and a sack of Bouncing Bulbs. The shock almost killed me; I was in bed for a week, and so deeply traumatised was I that I developed the habit of sleepwalking back to the same keyhole every night, until at last my dear papa, with only my best interests at heart, put a Sticking Charm on my door at bedtime.' Apparently Beatrix could find no way to make 'The Warlock's Hairy Heart' suitable for children's sensitive ears, as she never rewrote it for *The Toadstool Tales*.

hurt is as human as to breathe. Nevertheless, we wizards seem particularly prone to the idea that we can bend the nature of existence to our will. The young warlock[2] in this story, for instance, decides that falling in love would adversely affect his comfort and security. He sees love as a humiliation, a weakness, a drain on a person's emotional and material resources.

Of course, the centuries-old trade in love potions shows that our fictional wizard is hardly alone in seeking to control the unpredictable course of love. The search for a true love potion[3] continues to this day, but no such elixir has yet been created, and

---

2. [The term 'warlock' is a very old one. Although it is sometimes used as interchangeable with 'wizard', it originally denoted one learned in duelling and all martial magic. It was also given as a title to wizards who had performed feats of bravery, rather as Muggles were sometimes knighted for acts of valour. By calling the young wizard in this story a warlock, Beedle indicates that he has already been recognised as especially skilful at offensive magic. These days wizards use 'warlock' in one of two ways: to describe a wizard of unusually fierce appearance, or as a title denoting particular skill or achievement. Thus, Dumbledore himself was Chief Warlock of the Wizengamot. JKR]

3. Hector Dagworth-Granger, founder of the Most Extraordinary Society of Potioneers, explains: 'Powerful infatuations can be induced by the skilful potioneer, but never yet has anyone managed to create the truly unbreakable, eternal, unconditional attachment that alone can be called Love.'

leading potioneers doubt that it is possible.

The hero in this tale, however, is not even interested in a simulacrum of love that he can create or destroy at will. He wants to remain for ever uninfected by what he regards as a kind of sickness, and therefore performs a piece of Dark Magic that would not be possible outside a storybook: he locks away his own heart.

The resemblance of this action to the creation of a Horcrux has been noted by many writers. Although Beedle's hero is not seeking to avoid death, he is dividing what was clearly not meant to be divided – body and heart, rather than soul – and in doing so, he is falling foul of the first of Adalbert Waffling's Fundamental Laws of Magic:

> *Tamper with the deepest mysteries – the source of life, the essence of self – only if prepared for consequences of the most extreme and dangerous kind.*

And sure enough, in seeking to become super-human this foolhardy young man renders himself inhuman. The heart he has locked away slowly shrivels and grows hair, symbolising his own descent to beasthood. He is finally reduced to a violent animal who takes what he wants by force, and he dies in a futile attempt to regain what is now for ever beyond his reach – a human heart.

Though somewhat dated, the expression 'to have a hairy heart' has passed into everyday wizarding language to describe a cold or unfeeling witch or wizard. My maiden aunt, Honoria, always alleged that she called off her engagement to a wizard in the Improper Use of Magic Office because she discovered in time that 'he had a hairy heart'. (It was rumoured, however, that she actually discovered him in the act of fondling some Horklumps,[4] which she found deeply shocking.) More recently, the self-help book *The Hairy Heart: A Guide to Wizards Who Won't Commit*[5] has topped bestseller lists.

---

4. Horklumps are pink, bristly mushroom-like creatures. It is very difficult to see why anyone would want to fondle them. For further information, see *Fantastic Beasts and Where to Find Them*.

5. Not to be confused with *Hairy Snout, Human Heart*, a heart-rending account of one man's struggle with lycanthropy.

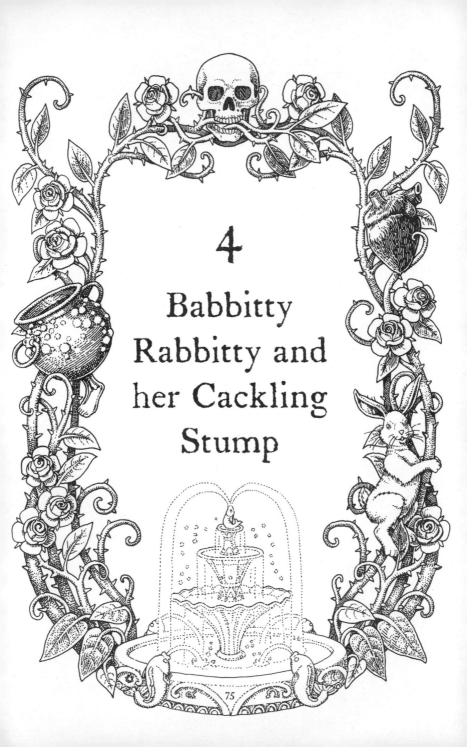

4

Babbitty Rabbitty and her Cackling Stump

A LONG TIME AGO, in a far-off land, there lived a foolish king who decided that he alone should have the power of magic.

He therefore commanded the head of his army to form a Brigade of Witch-Hunters, and issued them with a pack of ferocious black hounds. At the same time, the King caused proclamations to be read in every village and town across the land: 'Wanted by the King, an Instructor in Magic.'

No true witch or wizard dared volunteer for the post, for they were all in hiding from the Brigade of Witch-Hunters.

However, a cunning charlatan with no magical

power saw a chance of enriching himself, and arrived at the palace, claiming to be a wizard of enormous skill. The charlatan performed a few simple tricks, which convinced the foolish King of his magical powers, and was immediately appointed Grand Sorcerer in Chief, the King's Private Magic Master.

The charlatan bade the King give him a large sack of gold, so that he might purchase wands and other magical necessities. He also requested several large rubies, to be used in the casting of curative charms, and a silver chalice or two, for the storing and maturing of potions. All these things the foolish King supplied.

The charlatan stowed the treasure safely in his own house and returned to the palace grounds.

He did not know that he was being watched by an old woman who lived in a hovel on the edge of the grounds. Her name was Babbitty, and she was the washerwoman who kept the palace linens soft, fragrant and white. Peeping from behind her drying sheets, Babbitty saw the charlatan snap two twigs from one of the King's trees and disappear into the palace.

The charlatan gave one of the twigs to the King and assured him that it was a wand of tremendous power.

'It will only work, however,' said the charlatan, 'when you are worthy of it.'

Every morning the charlatan and the foolish King walked out into the palace grounds, where they waved their wands and shouted nonsense at the sky.

The charlatan was careful to perform more tricks, so that the King remained convinced of his Grand Sorcerer's skill, and of the power of the wands that had cost so much gold.

One morning, as the charlatan and the foolish King were twirling their twigs, and hopping in circles, and chanting meaningless rhymes, a loud cackling reached the King's ears. Babbitty the washerwoman was watching the King and the charlatan from the window of her tiny cottage, and was laughing so hard she soon sank out of sight, too weak to stand.

'I must look most undignified, to make the old washerwoman laugh so!' said the King. He ceased his hopping and twig twirling, and frowned. 'I grow weary of practice! When shall I be ready to perform real spells in front of my subjects, Sorcerer?'

The charlatan tried to soothe his pupil, assuring him that he would soon be capable of astonishing feats of magic, but Babbitty's cackling had stung the foolish King more than the charlatan knew.

'Tomorrow,' said the King, 'we shall invite our court to watch their King perform magic!

The charlatan saw that the time had come to take his treasure and flee.

'Alas, Your Majesty, it is impossible! I had forgotten to tell Your Majesty that I must set out on a long journey tomorrow –'

'If you leave this palace without my permission, Sorcerer, my Brigade of Witch-Hunters will hunt you down with their hounds! Tomorrow morning you will assist me to perform magic for the benefit of my lords and ladies, and if anybody laughs at me, I shall have you beheaded!'

The King stormed back to the palace, leaving the charlatan alone and afraid. Not all his cunning could save him now, for he could not run away, nor could he help the King with magic that neither of them knew.

Seeking a vent for his fear and his anger, the charlatan approached the window of Babbitty the washerwoman. Peering inside, he saw the little old lady sitting at her table, polishing a wand. In a corner behind her, the King's sheets were washing themselves in a wooden tub.

The charlatan understood at once that Babbitty was a true witch, and that she who had given him his awful problem could also solve it.

'Crone!' roared the charlatan. 'Your cackling has cost me dear! If you fail to help me, I shall denounce you as a witch, and it will be you who is torn apart by the King's hounds!'

Old Babbitty smiled at the charlatan and assured him that she would do everything in her power to help.

The charlatan instructed her to conceal herself

inside a bush while the King gave his magical display, and to perform the King's spells for him, without his knowledge. Babbitty agreed to the plan but asked one question.

'What, sir, if the King attempts a spell Babbitty cannot perform?'

The charlatan scoffed.

'Your magic is more than equal to that fool's imagination,' he assured her, and he retired to the castle, well pleased with his own cleverness.

The following morning all the lords and ladies of the kingdom assembled in the palace grounds. The King climbed on to a stage in front of them, with the charlatan by his side.

'I shall firstly make this lady's hat disappear!' cried the King, pointing his twig at a noblewoman.

From inside a bush nearby, Babbitty pointed her wand at the hat and caused it to vanish. Great was the astonishment and admiration of the crowd, and loud their applause for the jubilant King.

'Next, I shall make that horse fly!' cried the King, pointing his twig at his own steed.

From inside the bush, Babbitty pointed her wand at the horse and it rose high into the air.

The crowd was still more thrilled and amazed, and they roared their appreciation of their magical King.

'And now,' said the King, looking all around for an idea; and the Captain of his Brigade of Witch-Hunters ran forwards.

'Your Majesty,' said the Captain, 'this very morning, Sabre died of eating a poisonous toadstool! Bring him back to life, Your Majesty, with your wand!'

And the Captain heaved on to the stage the lifeless body of the largest of the witch-hunting hounds.

The foolish King brandished his twig and pointed it at the dead dog. But inside the bush, Babbitty smiled, and did not trouble to lift her wand, for no magic can raise the dead.

When the dog did not stir, the crowd began first to whisper, and then to laugh. They suspected that the King's first two feats had been mere tricks after all.

'Why doesn't it work?' the King screamed at the charlatan, who bethought himself of the only ruse left to him.

'There, Your Majesty, there!' he shouted, pointing at the bush where Babbitty sat concealed. 'I see her plain, a wicked witch who is blocking your magic with her own evil spells! Seize her, somebody, seize her!'

Babbitty fled from the bush, and the Brigade of Witch-Hunters set off in pursuit, unleashing their hounds, who bayed for Babbitty's blood. But as she

THE TALES OF BEEDLE THE BARD

reached a low hedge, the little witch vanished from sight, and when the King, the charlatan and all the courtiers gained the other side, they found the pack of witch-hunting hounds barking and scrabbling around a bent and aged tree.

'She has turned herself into a tree!' screamed the charlatan and, dreading lest Babbitty turn back into a woman and denounce him, he added, 'Cut her down, Your Majesty, that is the way to treat evil witches!'

An axe was brought at once, and the old tree was felled to loud cheers from the courtiers and the charlatan.

However, as they were making ready to return to the palace, the sound of loud cackling stopped them in their tracks.

'Fools!' cried Babbitty's voice from the stump they had left behind. 'No witch or wizard can be killed by being cut in half! Take the axe, if you do not believe me, and cut the Grand Sorcerer in two!'

The Captain of the Brigade of Witch-Hunters was eager to make the experiment, but as he raised the axe the charlatan fell to his knees, screaming for mercy and confessing all his wickedness. As he was dragged away to the dungeons, the tree stump cackled more loudly than ever.

'By cutting a witch in half, you have unleashed a dreadful curse upon your kingdom!' it told the petrified King. 'Henceforth, every stroke of harm that you inflict upon my fellow witches and wizards will feel like an axe stroke in your own side, until you will wish you could die of it!'

At that, the King fell to his knees too, and told the stump that he would issue a proclamation at once, protecting all the witches and wizards of the kingdom, and allowing them to practise their magic in peace.

'Very good,' said the stump, 'but you have not yet made amends to Babbitty!'

'Anything, anything at all!' cried the foolish King, wringing his hands before the stump.

'You will erect a statue of Babbitty upon me, in memory of your poor washerwoman, and to remind you for ever of your own foolishness!' said the stump.

The King agreed to it at once, and promised to engage the foremost sculptor in the land, and have the statue made of pure gold. Then the shamed King and all the noblemen and women returned to the palace, leaving the tree stump cackling behind them.

When the grounds were deserted once more, there wriggled from a hole between the roots of the tree stump a stout and whiskery old rabbit with a wand clamped between her teeth. Babbitty hopped out of the grounds and far away, and ever after a golden statue of the washerwoman stood upon the tree stump, and no witch or wizard was ever persecuted in the kingdom again.

Albus Dumbledore on 'Babbitty Rabbitty and her Cackling Stump'

The story of 'Babbitty Rabbitty and her Cackling Stump' is, in many ways, the most 'real' of Beedle's tales, in that the magic described in the story conforms, almost entirely, to known magical laws.

It was through this story that many of us first discovered that magic could not bring back the dead – and a great disappointment and shock it was, convinced as we had been, as young children, that our parents would be able to awaken our dead rats and cats with one wave of their wands. Though some six centuries have elapsed since Beedle wrote this tale, and while we have devised innumerable ways of maintaining the illusion of our loved ones' continuing presence,[1] wizards still have not found a way of reuniting body and soul once death has occurred. As the eminent wizarding philosopher Bertrand de Pensées-Profondes writes in his celebrated work *A Study into the Possibility of Reversing the Actual and Metaphysical Effects of Natural Death, with Particular Regard to the Reintegration of Essence and Matter*: 'Give it up. It's never going to happen.'

The tale of Babbitty Rabbitty does, however, give us one of the earliest literary mentions of an Animagus, for Babbitty the washerwoman is possessed of the rare magical ability to transform into an animal at will.

Animagi make up a small fraction of the wizarding

---

1. [Wizarding photographs and portraits move and (in the case of the latter) talk just like their subjects. Other rare objects, such as the Mirror of Erised, may also reveal more than a static image of a lost loved one. Ghosts are transparent, moving, talking and thinking versions of wizards and witches who wished, for whatever reason, to remain on earth. JKR]

population. Achieving perfect, spontaneous human to animal transformation requires much study and practice, and many witches and wizards consider that their time might be better employed in other ways. Certainly, the application of such a talent is limited unless one has a great need of disguise or concealment. It is for this reason that the Ministry of Magic has insisted upon a register of Animagi, for there can be no doubt that this kind of magic is of greatest use to those engaged in surreptitious, covert or even criminal activity.[2]

Whether there was ever a washerwoman who was able to transform into a rabbit is open to doubt; however, some magical historians have suggested that Beedle modelled Babbitty on the famous French sorceress Lisette de Lapin, who was convicted of witchcraft in Paris in 1422. To the astonishment of her Muggle guards, who were later tried for helping

---

2. [Professor McGonagall, Headmistress of Hogwarts, has asked me to make clear that she became an Animagus merely as a result of her extensive researches into all fields of Transfiguration, and that she has never used the ability to turn into a tabby cat for any surreptitious purpose, setting aside legitimate business on behalf of the Order of the Phoenix where secrecy and concealment were imperative. JKR]

the witch to escape, Lisette vanished from her prison cell the night before she was due to be executed. Although it has never been proven that Lisette was an Animagus who managed to squeeze through the bars of her cell window, a large white rabbit was subsequently seen crossing the English Channel in a cauldron with a sail fitted to it, and a similar rabbit later became a trusted advisor at the court of King Henry VI.[3]

The King in Beedle's story is a foolish Muggle who both covets and fears magic. He believes that he can become a wizard simply by learning incantations and waving a wand.[4] He is completely ignorant of the true nature of magic and wizards, and therefore

---

3. This may have contributed to that Muggle King's reputation for mental instability.

4. As intensive studies in the Department of Mysteries demonstrated as far back as 1672, wizards and witches are born, not created. While the 'rogue' ability to perform magic sometimes appears in those of apparent non-magical descent (though several later studies have suggested that there will have been a witch or wizard somewhere on the family tree), Muggles cannot perform magic. The best – or worst – they could hope for are random and uncontrollable effects generated by a genuine magical wand, which, as an instrument through which magic is supposed to be channelled, sometimes holds residual power that it may discharge at odd moments – see also the notes on wandlore for 'The Tale of the Three Brothers'.

swallows the preposterous suggestions of both the charlatan and Babbitty. This is certainly typical of a particular type of Muggle thinking: in their ignorance, they are prepared to accept all sorts of impossibilities about magic, including the proposition that Babbitty has turned herself into a tree that can still think and talk. (It is worth noting at this point, however, that while Beedle uses the talking-tree device to show us how ignorant the Muggle King is, he also asks us to believe that Babbitty can talk while she is a rabbit. This might be poetic licence, but I think it more likely that Beedle had only heard about Animagi, and never met one, for this is the only liberty that he takes with magical laws in the story. Animagi do not retain the power of human speech while in their animal form, although they keep all their human thinking and reasoning powers. This, as every schoolchild knows, is the fundamental difference between being an Animagus, and Transfiguring oneself into an animal. In the case of the latter, one would become the animal entirely, with the consequence that one would know no magic, be unaware that one had ever been a wizard, and would need somebody else to Transfigure one back to one's original form.)

I think it possible that in choosing to make his heroine pretend to turn into a tree, and threaten the King with pain like an axe stroke in his own side, Beedle was inspired by real magical traditions and practices. Trees with wand-quality wood have always been fiercely protected by the wandmakers who tend them, and cutting down such trees to steal them risks incurring not only the malice of the Bowtruckles[5] usually nesting there, but also the ill effect of any protective curses placed around them by their owners. In Beedle's time, the Cruciatus Curse had not yet been made illegal by the Ministry of Magic,[6] and could have produced precisely the sensation with which Babbitty threatens the King.

---

5. For a full description of these curious little tree-dwellers, see *Fantastic Beasts and Where to Find Them*.

6. The Cruciatus, Imperius and Avada Kedavra Curses were first classified as Unforgivable in 1717, with the strictest penalties attached to their use.

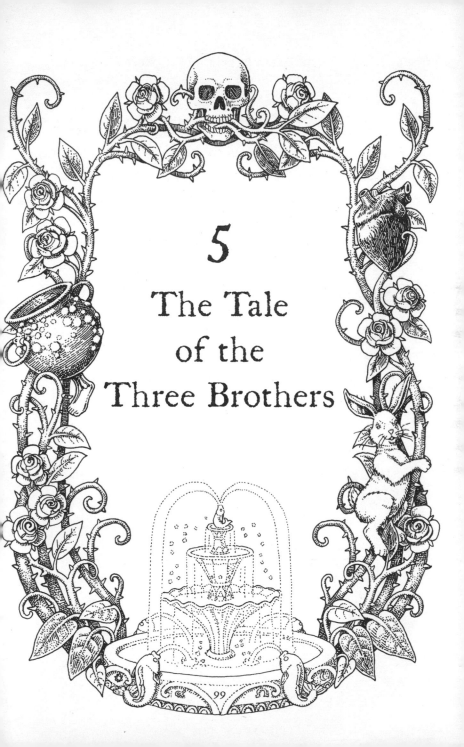

5

The Tale
of the
Three Brothers

THERE WERE ONCE THREE brothers who were travelling along a lonely, winding road at twilight. In time, the brothers reached a river too deep to wade through and too dangerous to swim across. However, these brothers were learned in the magical arts, and so they simply waved their wands and made a bridge appear across the treacherous water. They were halfway across it when they found their path blocked by a hooded figure.

And Death spoke to them. He was angry that he had been cheated out of three new victims, for travellers usually drowned in the river. But Death was cunning. He pretended to congratulate the three

brothers upon their magic, and said that each had earned a prize for having been clever enough to evade him.

So the oldest brother, who was a combative man, asked for a wand more powerful than any in existence: a wand that must always win duels for its owner, a wand worthy of a wizard who had conquered Death! So Death crossed to an elder tree on the banks of the river, fashioned a wand from a branch that hung there, and gave it to the oldest brother.

Then the second brother, who was an arrogant man, decided that he wanted to humiliate Death still further, and asked for the power to recall others from Death. So Death picked up a stone from the riverbank and gave it to the second brother, and told him that the stone would have the power to bring back the dead.

And then Death asked the third and youngest brother what he would like. The youngest brother was the humblest and also the wisest of the brothers, and he did not trust Death. So he asked for something that would enable him to go forth from that place without being followed by Death.

And Death, most unwillingly, handed over his own Cloak of Invisibility. Then Death stood aside and allowed the three brothers to continue on their way and they did so, talking with wonder of the adventure they had had, and admiring Death's gifts.

In due course the brothers separated, each for his own destination.

The first brother travelled on for a week or more, and reaching a distant village, he sought out a fellow wizard with whom he had a quarrel. Naturally, with the Elder Wand as his weapon, he could not fail to win the duel that followed. Leaving his enemy dead upon the floor, the oldest brother proceeded to an inn, where he boasted loudly of the powerful wand he had snatched from Death himself, and of how it made him invincible.

That very night, another wizard crept upon the oldest brother as he lay, wine-sodden, upon his bed. The thief took the wand and, for good measure, slit the oldest brother's throat.

And so Death took the first brother for his own.

Meanwhile, the second brother journeyed to his own home, where he lived alone. Here he took out the stone that had the power to recall the dead, and turned it thrice in his hand. To his amazement and his delight, the figure of the girl he had once hoped to marry before her untimely death appeared at once before him.

Yet she was
silent and cold,
separated from him as
though by a veil. Though
she had returned to the
mortal world, she did not
truly belong there and
suffered. Finally, the
second brother, driven
mad with hopeless long-
ing, killed himself so
as truly to join her.

And so Death
took the second
brother for his
own.

But though Death searched for the third brother for many years, he was never able to find him. It was only when he had attained a great age that the youngest brother finally took off the Cloak of Invisibility and gave it to his son. And then he greeted Death as an old friend, and went with him gladly, and, equals, they departed this life.

Albus Dumbledore on 'The Tale of the Three Brothers'

This story made a profound impression on me as a boy. I heard it first from my mother, and it soon became the tale I requested more often than any other at bedtime. This frequently led to arguments with my younger brother, Aberforth, whose favourite story was 'Grumble the Grubby Goat'.

The moral of 'The Tale of the Three Brothers' could not be any clearer:

human efforts to evade or overcome death are always doomed to disappointment. The third brother in the story ('the humblest and also the wisest') is the only one who understands that, having narrowly escaped Death once, the best he can hope for is to postpone their next meeting for as long as possible. This youngest brother knows that taunting Death – by engaging in violence, like the first brother, or by meddling in the shadowy art of necromancy,[1] like the second brother – means pitting oneself against a wily enemy who cannot lose.

The irony is that a curious legend has grown up around this story, which precisely contradicts the message of the original. This legend holds that the gifts Death gives the brothers – an unbeatable wand, a stone that can bring back the dead, and an Invisibility Cloak that endures for ever – are genuine objects that exist in the real world. The legend goes further: if any person becomes the rightful owner of all three, then he or she will

---

1. [Necromancy is the Dark Art of raising the dead. It is a branch of magic that has never worked, as this story makes clear. JKR]

become 'master of Death', which has usually been understood to mean that they will be invulnerable, even immortal.

We may smile, a little sadly, at what this tells us about human nature. The kindest interpretation would be: 'Hope springs eternal'.[2] In spite of the fact that, according to Beedle, two of the three objects are highly dangerous, in spite of the clear message that Death comes for us all in the end, a tiny minority of the wizarding community persists in believing that Beedle was sending them a coded message, which is the exact reverse of the one set down in ink, and that they alone are clever enough to understand it.

Their theory (or perhaps 'desperate hope' might be a more accurate term) is supported by little actual evidence. True Invisibility Cloaks, though rare, exist in this world of ours; however, the story makes it clear that Death's Cloak is of a uniquely durable

---

2. [This quotation demonstrates that Albus Dumbledore was not only exceptionally well read in wizarding terms, but also that he was familiar with the writings of Muggle poet Alexander Pope. JKR]

nature.3 Through all the centuries that have
intervened between Beedle's day and our own,
nobody has ever claimed to have found Death's
Cloak. This is explained away by true believers thus:
either the third brother's descendants do not know
where their Cloak came from, or they know and are
determined to show their ancestor's wisdom by not
trumpeting the fact.

Naturally enough, the stone has never been
found, either. As I have already noted in the
commentary for 'Babbitty Rabbitty and her Cackling
Stump', we remain incapable of raising the dead,
and there is every reason to suppose that this will
never happen. Vile substitutions have, of course,
been attempted by Dark wizards, who have created
Inferi,4 but these are ghastly puppets, not truly

---

3. [Invisibility Cloaks are not, generally, infallible. They may rip or
grow opaque with age, or the charms placed upon them may wear off,
or be countered by charms of revealment. This is why witches and
wizards usually turn, in the first instance, to Disillusionment Charms for
self-camouflage or concealment. Albus Dumbledore was known to be able to
perform a Disillusionment Charm so powerful as to render himself invisible
without the need for a Cloak. JKR]

4. [Inferi are corpses reanimated by Dark Magic. JKR]

reawoken humans. What is more, Beedle's story is quite explicit about the fact that the second brother's lost love has not really returned from the dead. She has been sent by Death to lure the second brother into Death's clutches, and is therefore cold, remote, tantalisingly both present and absent.[5]

This leaves us with the wand, and here the obstinate believers in Beedle's hidden message have at least some historical evidence to back up their wild claims. For it is the case – whether because they liked to glorify themselves, or to intimidate possible attackers, or because they truly believed what they were saying – that wizards down the ages have claimed to possess a wand more powerful than the ordinary, even an 'unbeatable' wand. Some of these wizards have gone so far as to claim that their wand is made of elder, like the wand supposedly made by Death. Such wands have been given many names, among them 'the Wand of Destiny' and 'the Deathstick'.

---

5. Many critics believe that Beedle was inspired by the Philosopher's Stone, which makes the immortality-inducing Elixir of Life, when creating this stone that can raise the dead.

It is hardly surprising that old superstitions have grown up around our wands, which are, after all, our most important magical tools and weapons. Certain wands (and therefore their owners) are supposed to be incompatible:

> *When his wand's oak and hers is holly,*
> *Then to marry would be folly.*

or to denote flaws in the owner's character:

> *Rowan gossips, chestnut drones,*
> *Ash is stubborn, hazel moans.*

And sure enough, within this category of unproven sayings we find:

> *Wand of elder, never prosper.*

Whether because of the fact that Death makes the fictional wand out of elder in Beedle's story, or because power-hungry or violent wizards have persistently claimed that their own wands are made of elder, it is not a wood that is much favoured among wandmakers.

The first well-documented mention of a wand made of elder that had particularly strong and dangerous powers was owned by Emeric, commonly called 'the Evil', a short-lived but exceptionally aggressive wizard who terrorised the South of England in the early Middle Ages. He died as he had lived, in a ferocious duel with a wizard known as Egbert. What became of Egbert is unknown, although the life expectancy of medieval duellers was generally short. In the days before there was a Ministry of Magic to regulate the use of Dark Magic, duelling was usually fatal.

A full century later, another unpleasant character, this time named Godelot, advanced the study of Dark Magic by writing a collection of dangerous spells with the help of a wand he described in his notebook as 'my moste wicked and subtle friend, with bodie of Ellhorn,[6] who knowes ways of magick

---

6. An old name for 'elder'.

moste evile'. (*Magick Moste Evile* became the title of Godelot's masterwork.)

As can be seen, Godelot considers his wand to be a helpmeet, almost an instructor. Those who are knowledgeable about wandlore[7] will agree that wands do indeed absorb the expertise of those who use them, though this is an unpredictable and imperfect business; one must consider all kinds of additional factors, such as the relationship between the wand and the user, to understand how well it is likely to perform with any particular individual. Nevertheless, a hypothetical wand that had passed through the hands of many Dark wizards would be likely to have, at the very least, a marked affinity for the most dangerous kinds of magic.

Most witches and wizards prefer a wand that has 'chosen' them to any kind of second-hand wand, precisely because the latter is likely to have learned habits from its previous owner that might not be compatible with the new user's style of magic. The

---

7. Such as myself.

general practice of burying (or burning) the wand with its owner, once he or she has died, also tends to prevent any individual wand learning from too many masters. Believers in the Elder Wand, however, hold that because of the way in which it has always passed allegiance between owners – the next master overcoming the first, usually by killing him – the Elder Wand has never been destroyed or buried, but has survived to accumulate wisdom, strength and power far beyond the ordinary.

Godelot is known to have perished in his own cellar, where he was locked by his mad son, Hereward. We must assume that Hereward took his father's wand, or the latter would have been able to escape, but what Hereward did with the wand after that we cannot be sure. All that is certain is that a wand called 'the Eldrun[8] Wand' by its owner, Barnabas Deverill, appeared in the early eighteenth century, and that Deverill used it to carve himself out a reputation as a fearsome warlock, until

---

8. Also an old name for 'elder'.

his reign of terror was ended by the equally notorious Loxias, who took the wand, rechristened it 'the Deathstick', and used it to lay waste to anyone who displeased him. It is difficult to trace the subsequent history of Loxias's wand, as many claimed to have finished him off, including his own mother.

What must strike any intelligent witch or wizard on studying the so-called history of the Elder Wand is that every man who claims to have owned it[9] has insisted that it is 'unbeatable', when the known facts of its passage through many owners' hands demonstrate that not only has it been beaten hundreds of times, but that it also attracts trouble as Grumble the Grubby Goat attracted flies. Ultimately, the quest for the Elder Wand merely supports an observation I have had occasion to make many times over the course of my long life: that humans have a knack of choosing precisely those things that are worst for them.

---

9. No witch has ever claimed to own the Elder Wand. Make of that what you will.

But which of us would have shown the wisdom of the third brother, if offered the pick of Death's gifts? Wizards and Muggles alike are imbued with a lust for power; how many would resist 'the Wand of Destiny'? Which human being, having lost someone they loved, could withstand the temptation of the Resurrection Stone? Even I, Albus Dumbledore, would find it easiest to refuse the Invisibility Cloak; which only goes to show that, clever as I am, I remain just as big a fool as anyone else.

LUMOS

Protecting Children. Providing Solutions.

A MESSAGE FROM GEORGETTE MULHEIR, CEO, LUMOS

Lumos (noun; lu-mos):

> *1. A spell to create light, also known as the Wand-Lighting Charm. (Origin: the Harry Potter series)*
> *2. A nonprofit working to end the institutionalisation of children.*

It all started with a photograph.

When J.K. Rowling saw the black-and-white image of a small boy – isolated, locked away from the world, away from his family and placed in an institution – she couldn't look away.

Now multiply that boy by eight million.

That's how many children there are worldwide who spend their early years in these residential institutions –

essentially orphanages. Only these children aren't orphans; they are loved and wanted by their families. But they're born into poverty, or with a disability, or they're from an ethnic minority, in a place where no support is offered.

What we at Lumos have discovered and put into practice is revolutionary: it is less expensive and more successful to shut orphanages and instead redirect their funds towards community-based solutions that support children in their homes, where they belong.

HOW DID WE GET HERE?

Over the past decades, orphanages have become the default response for many a vulnerable child and family. Often it is the only option offered to desperate parents. And the impact is devastating and profoundly affects their chances in life.

Research shows they are at a greater risk of being trafficked and of suffering from various forms of abuse and neglect. Further, as adults they struggle to cope in the outside world.

LIGHTING A PATH TOWARDS REAL CHANGE

For our world to prosper, we need to make sure all children don't just survive, but thrive. Lumos focuses on the key ingredient that offers children the *emotional* sustenance they require: the individual love and care provided by parents.

Research into the early brain development of infants shows that it is the individual attention, responsiveness, and stimulation provided by consistent parenting – and the consequent attachment formed between child and parent – that helps the brain grow and develop. In essence, the bond between parent and child is the root from which all success, all well-being, grows.

Although orphanages are established with the best of intentions, no matter how hard the care staff try, they cannot replicate a family. There are too few staff caring for too many children, leaving them alone for hours without stimulation – or even simple human contact.

Thankfully, this is an entirely solvable problem. Many countries around the world have moved away from looking after children in orphanages and, instead, provide a range of supports that make it possible to keep children in families included in their communities.

A GLOBAL ORGANISATION

Our work has helped achieve a tipping point in the European

region: the European Union and other big donors now understand that orphanages are not the answer and have redirected their funds towards community-based services.

Placing children with their families where they belong is no longer a question of if, but rather when and how.

But across the world, many countries still use orphanages to ostensibly meet the needs of vulnerable children. Lumos is helping to lead a global effort to reverse this trend. By implementing programmes that demonstrate how effective the Lumos model is and by influencing the world's decision-makers to support children in families and not orphanages, we'll see the changes we've made in Europe filter through the rest of the world.

A GLOBAL MOVEMENT

Changing the status quo will take time, political and public will, and a concerted effort to challenge the disconnect between the perception of orphanages and their reality:

- Orphanages are not full of orphans – they are filled with children who have loving families but just need support.

- Many are not benign or necessary places for children in adversity.
- They do not provide the best outcomes for children.
- They are not the most cost-effective solution.

By buying this unique and special book, you are helping Lumos to make sure that, by 2050, no more children live in institutions around the world, and together, we can consign orphanages to the history books, where they belong.

Together, we can refocus the world's efforts towards supporting children and families where they live, in their own homes and communities.

Together, we can cast a bit of light to cut through the darkness.

Together, we are Lumos.

You are invited to share the magic of

HARRY
POTTER
BOOK
NIGHT

To find out how you can join in the fun, visit

harrypotterbooknight.com

FOR GAMES, COMPETITIONS,
AND FUN DOWNLOADS
VISIT

harrypotter.bloomsbury.com